Francesca Bosca

CASPAR and the STAR

Translated by Philip Hawthorn
Illustrations by Giuliano Ferri

A LION PICTURE STORY
Oxford · Batavia · Sydney

Caspar was a wise and clever man who lived in a tiny house perched on the top of a hill.

Every night he could be seen gazing up at the sky, for the study of the stars was the love of his life.

As soon as the first stars appeared in the evening sky, Caspar would hurry outside and gaze at them in wide-eyed wonder.

During the day Caspar would read book after book, only lifting his head to watch for the darkening of the evening sky. Then he would smile— sitting by the window, waiting amid the silence of a thousand thoughts.

Then suddenly, one evening, the silence was broken: "It's here! It's come! At last the star has arrived!"

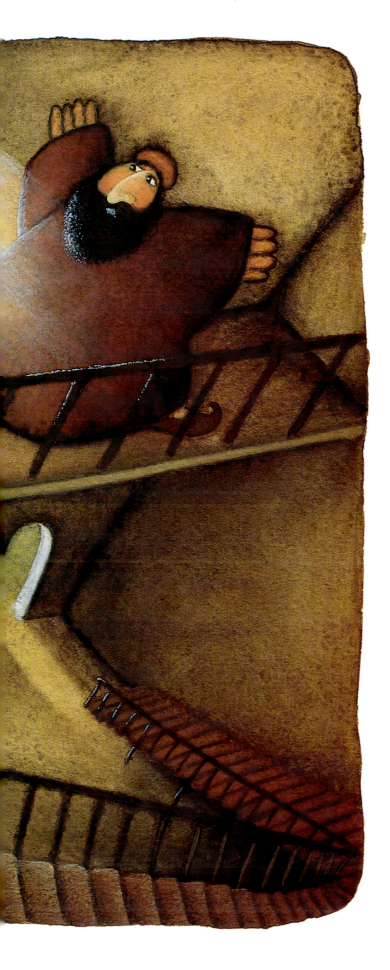

Shouting and waving his arms above his head, Caspar ran outside, bursting with joy. The star for which he had been waiting so long was there right in front of him—and it was more beautiful and majestic than any star he had ever seen before.

He decided that he must begin his journey at once. So, packing everything he needed, he left his house and set off. He wouldn't need a map: this special star would show him the way—the way to a very special baby.

Caspar followed the star for many nights until he found himself in front of the most wonderful palace. It had hundreds of turrets, and the walls were covered with glittering jewels.

He stopped and stared in amazement: the palace was so resplendent that it lit up the dark night sky.

The star had also stopped, and so Caspar thought that he had reached the end of his journey.

Next morning, inside the palace, Caspar met a man called Melchior. He also loved to study the stars and the two men were soon talking like old friends. Caspar told him all about his journey and the star that he was following.

Smiling broadly, Melchior replied: "I also am here to look for the baby, and I think I have found him. Someone told me that a few days ago the queen gave birth to her first son. Perhaps this is the baby for whom we are searching!"

Together they went to the royal court and asked if they could see the baby.

As they entered the room, Caspar's heart began to beat faster.

"Do you remember what the ancient books told us?" he whispered. "He is the one who will bring joy and peace to all the world. He will comfort the poor and the sad—and kings and queens will bow down before him."

"Yes, this must be him," replied Melchior.

But they were wrong. For just then, something in the sky caught their eye: it was the star, moving away from the palace.

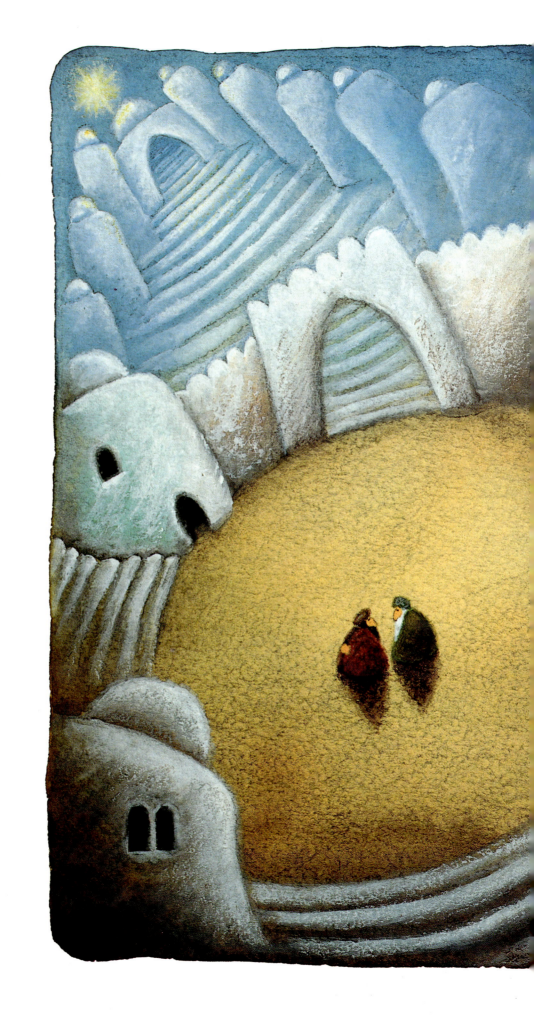

So Caspar and Melchior
set off on their journey
once more, faithfully
following the star. After a few
days it stopped again, having
led them to a city that was so
beautiful, the two friends were
left absolutely speechless.

But this was no time for sightseeing—they hurried off in search of the baby. Inside the king's palace they met a man called Balthazar, and they told him all about their adventure.

"You won't believe it," replied Balthazar, "but I've been following the star as well! I also want to find this baby—my books have spoken so much about him." Then he lowered his voice and continued with great excitement: "I've heard that the king and queen here have recently had a son—let's go and see him!"

As they looked at the baby, Melchior remembered what his books had promised: "He will be a great king. He will bring his people out of the land of darkness into the kingdom of light."

"Just look at him, surely he is our king!" exclaimed Balthazar.

But once more the star had begun to move on its continuing journey.

At once the three wise men also left the city and followed the way that the star showed them.

But now their faces were full of sadness. Maybe their books had not told the truth, or maybe this star was not the one they were supposed to follow?

The three wise men rode along in silence for mile after weary mile, each of them wrapped up in his own thoughts.

Soon they noticed that even the star had abandoned them: it had suddenly disappeared. Now their troubled hearts became even heavier with doubts and questions.

"Maybe the time has come for us to turn back," sighed Caspar, with bitter disappointment.

But just at that moment Balthazar interrupted him.

"Look, you two! I can see lights—down there!" he said, pointing excitedly. "It's a city! Perhaps we'll find someone there who can give us some answers."

Their hopes rose again as they approached the city of Jerusalem.

The following day, news of the three strangers reached the court of King Herod, a powerful and cruel man. Herod was very worried by what he heard, so he brought together all his advisers.

"There are three men in the city asking about the birth of a baby," he said, frowning. "They say he will be king of all people. What does all this mean—who is this baby?"

Herod's advisers could only confirm his fears: their books also told about the coming of a very special baby. But Herod would not listen to them.

"I am the only king around here!" he boomed, "and I will protect my throne at all costs—even if I have to kill to do it!"

Herod banged his fist down, almost cracking his throne. Then he smiled, and said: "Invite these strangers to the palace. I'd like a little chat with them."

Caspar, Melchior and
Balthazar gladly
accepted Herod's
invitation; at last someone
might be able to help them.
However, once they were
standing in front of him, their
enthusiasm gradually began to
trickle away. Herod gave no
answers at all, he only asked
question after question. He
asked them about each and
every detail of their journey
and what they hoped to find.

As he wished them farewell,
he said: "Go and search for the
baby, and when you have found
him, let me know so that I can
also go and . . . worship him!"

The three wise men left the palace, very disturbed by this strange meeting. Herod did not seem to be as happy or excited about the baby's coming as they were. What did he really want?

That evening, feeling puzzled and confused, the three wise men left Jerusalem. Then, after journeying for many cold, dark hours, they saw the faint glow of a small fire in the middle of a clearing.

As they drew nearer they noticed, seated near the fire, a shepherd who was keeping a watch on his flock. Without hesitation he invited the three strangers to sit down and warm themselves.

Caspar, Melchior and Balthazar told the shepherd the story of their long journey. He thought for a moment, then said: "The other day I came upon a strange sight. At Bethlehem, it was. A couple with a tiny baby—just been born, he had—and they'd put him in a manger. Someone said he was a king! Well, there were no armies or servants around him, but even so his little face made me so happy and . . . peaceful. I felt special just to be there."

The three wise men looked at each other, then they eagerly asked the shepherd to take them to the place and show them this baby. Along the way the star appeared once more, shining more brightly than ever—just like the hope in their hearts.

When they arrived, Caspar, Melchior and Balthazar knelt down beside the baby. They tingled with a new joy that made them want to stay and worship him for ever.

At last they had found the King of Love—and their real journey had just begun.

Original text and illustrations copyright © 1991
Edizioni Paoline srl, Cinisello Balsamo (Italy)
Translation copyright © 1991 Lion Publishing

Published by
Lion Publishing plc
Sandy Lane West, Oxford, England
ISBN 0 7459 2120 5
Lion Publishing Corporation
1705 Hubbard Avenue, Batavia, Illinois 60510, USA
ISBN 0 7459 2120 5
Albatross Books Pty Ltd
PO Box 320, Sutherland, NSW 2232, Australia
ISBN 0 7324 0505 X

First edition published 1991 under the title *Cammina,
cammina...* by Edizioni Paoline
First English edition 1991 Lion Publishing

British Library and Library of Congress CIP data
applied for

Printed and bound in Singapore